The Twelve Animals
of the
Chinese Zodiac

Traditional Fables in Chinese and English
十二生肖的民间故事

Vivian Ling and Wang Peng

Illustrated by Yang Xi

TUTTLE Publishing

Tokyo | Rutland, Vermont | Singapore

Contents

A Letter to All Readers Young and Old

Welcome to the land of fables, a place inhabited by all kinds of creatures who think and talk like humans! You have probably been here before, but I'd bet you will find some fun characters in these pages that you have never met before.

Nowadays we think of fables as stories for kids. But actually, long before they became children's stories, they were serious stuff for grown-ups. In fact, they appeared in many ancient texts like the Bible and the Chinese classics. Fables have been popular around the world since ancient times, not just because they were fun stories, but also because they made it easy to learn important lessons about life.

Nobody likes being told what to do, especially people in powerful positions or smart alecks who are too proud for their own good. How would you feel if your Dad scolded you for slacking off just because you are smart? But wasn't it fun to hear the story about how a slow turtle beat a speedy hare in a race when the hare decided to take a break? Similarly, a king in ancient China had two ministers, a loyal one and an evil one, but he stupidly favored the evil one. The loyal minister couldn't very well warn the king by saying "That evil minister is stealing your power," so he made up the story about the fox and the tiger, and said at the end, "See how the tiger lost his might to the fox?" This story became an all-time favorite in China, and it appears on page 24 in this book.

In Western culture, Aesop the Greek is considered the founding father of fables. The remarkable thing about Aesop is that he was a slave, the lowest class of people in society. By creating fabulous fables, he transformed himself from a voiceless lowly person into the most beloved storyteller. He was so successful that his works were imitated, and other fabulists pretended their works were his. To honor Aesop's gift to the world, we will present some of his stories in this book.

Somewhere along the way, fables became a favorite kind of stories for kids as well, but their original serious purpose never changed. How could something that serious be so much fun at the same time? Well, fables tend to be brief, simple, and short, but these little nuggets pack a lot of wit and wisdom. They also assume that you the reader are very smart. So they don't tell the whole story, just enough for you to figure out the "secrets" that lie behind the words. This way, you are the co-creator of the story. When you come to the end of a fable, don't just slam the book shut and say "so what?!" Instead, ask yourself, "so...?," and then give yourself all the time you need for the good ideas to bubble up from inside of you.

Just as the world is always changing, a good fable needs to be renewed if it's to retain its charm. If you come across stories in this book that you know, but are not exactly like how you remembered them, it's not because we got the stories wrong, it's because we deliberately tweaked them to be more in tune with with readers today. Enjoy!

Your friends,
Vivian Ling, **Wang Peng**, and **Yang Xi**

How the Twelve Animals Won Their Places in the Chinese Zodiac

In Western culture, a good way to show your relatives and friends that you care about them is to remember their birthdays. The Chinese do the same thing by remembering people's "birthyears." That's because the Chinese have a "zodiac" that gives meaning to each birthyear, which makes a Chinese person feel special. In traditional China, everybody was considered to be one year older on Lunar New Year, as though they all just had a birthday.

十二生肖的故事

在西方文化里，记住亲朋好友的生日表示你关爱他们。中国人也一样，不过他们大多记得的是亲朋好友出生在哪一年。因为"十二生肖"里的每一年各有特色，每个人也因此感到很独特。照中国的传统文化，每个人在农历新年的时候就都长了一岁，好像这一天大家都过了生日。

The Chinese way of remembering birthyears was invented by the legendary Jade Emperor. He came up with the idea of a zodiac cycle of 12 years, each one represented by a certain animal. If you can remember which zodiac animal a friend belongs to, then it's easy to figure out the year he was born and then his age. People born 12 years apart, or any multiples of 12 years, belong to the same zodiac animal. For example, the year 2020 was the year of the Mouse, so everyone born in 2020, as well as in 1996, 2008, 2032, and 2044 belongs to the Mouse.

传说中，玉皇大帝发明了一个帮助人们记住出生年份的方法。他想出了十二生肖的主意，就用一种动物来代表一个生肖，也叫做属相。要是你记得一个朋友的属相是什么，那就很容易算出他是哪一年出生的，他的年龄多大。两个出生年份相隔12年的人，或是出生在12倍数年份的人都是同一个属相。比方说，2020年是鼠年，凡是出生在2020年，或是1996年、2008年、2032年以及2044年的人都属鼠。

After the Jade Emperor decided on a cycle of 12 years, he had to think of a way to choose 12 animals to fill the 12 spots in the zodiac. So he decided to hold a contest. At the set date and time, all the animals who wished to be chosen by the Jade Emperor may present their best selves in front of his palace.

　　玉皇大帝确定了十二生肖以后，接下来就得选12种动物了。他决定举办一场生肖竞选大赛。在大赛选定的日子和钟点，所有希望被玉皇大帝选上的动物都可以在皇宫前接受检阅。

The Cow, a diligent animal that always got up at the crack of dawn, was the first one to arrive that morning. But along the way, she came to a creek. The Mouse ran right behind her and asked if he may hitch a ride on her back to cross the creek. Being big-hearted, the Cow said "Sure! Hop on!" After crossing the creek, the Mouse decided that wasn't enough; he wanted to get a free ride for the rest of the way! Again, the Cow agreed.

在举办大赛的那一天，习惯一大早就辛勤劳动的牛是第一个到达的。不过，牠在去参赛的路上正要过一条小溪的时候，鼠突然从后面跑了上来，问能不能骑在牠的背上渡过小溪。牛很大方地说："当然可以，上来吧！"过了小溪以后，鼠不想下来了，又问牛能不能一直把牠载到比赛现场，牛也同意了。

From early that morning, the Jade Emperor waited in front of his palace for the animals to arrive. When he saw the Cow approaching, he was ready to name her the first animal of the zodiac. But the Mouse immediately saw an opportunity. He hopped off the Cow's back and landed right in front of her. The Jade Emperor was so impressed with his cleverness that he named him the first in the zodiac. The big-hearted Cow was bumped down to second place, which she didn't mind at all.

生肖竞赛日的大清早，玉皇大帝就在宫殿前等待着动物们的到来。他看见牛走近了，正要把牛定为十二生肖第一名的时候，鼠看见机会来了，就从牛背上飞身而下，跳到了牛的前面。玉皇大帝看见这个机灵的鼠，就决定把鼠排在了十二生肖的第一位。宽厚的牛只好落到了第二位，不过牠一点儿也不介意。

Close behind them came the Tiger and the Rabbit. The Jade Emperor was very taken with the Tiger's stripes and the Rabbit's perky ears, so he named them number three and number four. By this time, quite a few other animals had arrived, and a crowd was beginning to gather. This made the Jade Emperor realize he'd better slow down and really look over all the contestants.

紧跟在牛和鼠后面到来的是虎和兔。玉皇大帝很欣赏虎身上的虎纹和兔的长耳朵，就把她们俩分别排在了第三位和第四位。这时候，动物们纷纷到了，大家聚在了一起，玉皇大帝看到眼前的情景，就觉得他得好好地筛选一下这群竞赛选手了。

As he looked up, he saw an amazing creature that looked a bit like a snake, only much bigger. Its head was like a lion; its body had scales like a fish; and it glided through the air without wings! The Jade Emperor called him to come forward to introduce himself. "Your Majesty, you have never seen me before because I am not from the animal kingdom. I was invented by the Chinese people, and they named me the Dragon." The Jade Emperor found him so charming that he not only placed him in the zodiac immediately, but also asked him if he had brought a relative along. When the Snake heard this, he quickly slithered forward and said, "Me, I'm the Dragon's godson!" And that's how the Snake became the sixth animal in the zodiac.

玉皇大帝抬头往前方看，发现了一个有点神奇的家伙，看起来有点像蛇，但个头大得多。这家伙的头有点像狮子，身上有鱼一样的鳞片；牠没有翅膀，但从空中滑翔而来！玉皇大帝招呼这家伙到前面来做自我介绍。"陛下，您从前没见过我，因为我不是动物王国的成员，而是中国神话里的动物，中国人把我叫做龙。"玉皇大帝听了很惊喜，立刻把龙定为十二生肖的第五位，还问龙有没有带一位亲戚一同来参赛。蛇听见这话，嘶地一下串到前面来说"我呀，我是龙的干儿子！"就这样，蛇就成为了十二生肖的第六位了。

With only half of the spots remaining, all the animals in the crowd began to get nervous, and some of them started to get pushy. But the Jade Emperor caught sight of the Horse and the Sheep bowing and making room for each other to move forward. Their politeness so impressed the Jade Emperor that he chose them to be the next two animals of the zodiac.

现在只剩下六个空位了，所有的动物都紧张了起来，有的甚至要争斗起来了。不过玉皇大帝看见马和羊在互相礼让，请对方往前挪步。看到牠们那么礼貌客气，玉皇大帝很开心，就把马和羊排在了十二生肖的第七位和第八位了。

The Monkey had a late start that day, so she was at the back of the crowd. But she was the most clever and nimble animal at the contest that day. Catching sight of a cloud floating by, she leaped up to grab the edge of it and swung herself to the front of the crowd. This amazing act made everyone—including the Jade Emperor—drop their jaw. So that's how the Monkey won the ninth spot.

猴那天出发得很晚，所以到了比赛场地也只能站在大伙儿的后头。不过牠是动物群里最聪明机灵的。看见一朵慢慢飘过来的云，猴轻轻一跳，抓住了云边儿，再一跃就跳到了最前边。这个动作让同伴们和玉皇大帝都惊掉了下巴。第九位理所当然就成了猴了。

At this point, the Rooster let out the loudest "cock-a-doodle-doo" of his life. The Jade Emperor realized that he could use someone like that to wake everybody up in the morning, so the Rooster was named number ten. This gave the Dog an idea: he stepped forward and offered to guard the Emperor's palace, and that's how he became number eleven.

这时候，公鸡使劲儿叫出了牠这一生最响亮的"呃喔——呃喔喔"，让玉皇大帝想到他真的需要公鸡在每天清晨唤醒睡梦中的人们，所以鸡就被选为第十位了。狗立刻从公鸡那儿得到了灵感，抢到前面自告奋勇地说牠愿意守卫皇宫，于是狗就成了第十一位。

By now, with only one spot left and so many wonderful animals competing for it, the Jade Emperor really didn't know what to do. So he blindfolded himself and went "eeny, meeny, miny, mo." When he opened his eyes, he was shocked to see that his finger was pointing at the Pig! But being a man of his word, he calmed himself and said politely, "What the heck, Piggy, you deserve this as much as anybody else!"

只剩下最后一个位子了，但还有那么多可爱的动物要竞赛呢，这可真让玉皇大帝为难。他只好蒙上了眼睛，开始点兵点将。等他睁开眼睛的时候，有点惊讶地发现手指点到的是猪！不过，玉皇大帝毕竟是个很守信用的人，所以平和又客气地说："好吧，猪儿，你跟别人一样配得上这个机会！"

Many of the contestants were disappointed that day, but they were all good sports about it. After all, the twelve animals that won spots in the zodiac did put on a great show for everyone. To honor the 12 winners and to thank the many more losers, the Jade Emperor invited everybody into the palace for a big feast, and everyone had a fabulous time.

很多落选的动物都很失望，但大家也很有风度地接受了，毕竟选上的12种动物都有精彩的表现。为了表彰选上的12种动物，也为了感谢大家的参与，玉皇大帝给大家办了个盛大的宴会。所有的动物都在宫殿里狂欢了一番！

How the Mouse Turned His Friend the Cat into a Mortal Enemy

We all know that mice are afraid of cats, but they were not always that way. Before the zodiac contest, the Cat and the Mouse were best friends. When the contest was announced, both of them became very excited and began making plans. The night before the contest, the Cat wanted to get a good night's sleep but was afraid she wouldn't be able to wake up in time. So, she asked her friend the Mouse to wake her up in the morning, in exchange for carrying the Mouse on her back. The Mouse thought this was a good deal, because he usually stayed up through the night anyway. But early next morning, just as the Mouse was about to go wake up the Cat, he thought "Cat might beat me in the contest!" So he decided to let the Cat sleep late and miss the contest.

猫鼠成冤家

人人都知道老鼠怕猫，但一开始并不是这样的。在十二生肖被选定以前，猫跟老鼠是最好的朋友。玉皇大帝要举办生肖大赛的消息公布以后，猫和老鼠都很兴奋，开始积极地做准备。大赛的前一天晚上，猫想好好睡上一觉，但是又怕自己早上睡过头。于是，猫请好朋友老鼠早上来叫醒牠，并答应第二天背着老鼠一起去参加生肖大赛。老鼠觉得这个主意对牠来说很合算，反正自己多半整个晚上都不睡觉。可是第二天一大早，老鼠正要去叫醒猫的时候，突然转念一想，"我很有可能在生肖大赛上比不过猫呢！"这样一想，老鼠决定让猫继续呼呼大睡，最好错过生肖大赛。

On the way to the contest, the Mouse hitched a ride with the Cow, and they ended up being the first and second ones chosen by the Jade Emperor. Before long, all twelve places of the zodiac were filled up. Afterwards, the wise Jade Emperor invited all the animals that showed up for the contest to a party, so that those who did not win would not go away feeling too disappointed.

在去参加生肖大赛的路上，老鼠遇见了牛，就骑在牛背上一起赶到了比赛地点，而玉皇大帝就把老鼠和牛选为十二生肖里的第一名和第二名。不一会儿，十二生肖就都选定了。接下来，玉皇大帝为所有来参加大赛的动物们举办了热闹的庆祝大会，这样的话，没有被选上的动物也就不会太失望了。

Meanwhile, the Cat slept on and on and on, until she was finally awakened by the rowdy animals returning from the big party. When she realized that the Mouse had tricked her into sleeping through the contest, she was furious. Then when she found out that the Mouse came in first, she wanted to catch him and tear him into bits!

庆祝大会终于结束了，回到家的动物们叽叽喳喳地谈论着，才把呼呼大睡的猫吵醒了。这时候，猫才发现自己被老鼠骗了。这可把牠气坏了！接着又发现老鼠甚至被选为十二生肖里的第一名，那牠简直气炸了，恨不得马上抓住老鼠，把牠咬成碎末！

Right then and there, the Cat and the Mouse became mortal enemies. To this day, the Mouse carries a guilty conscience and runs for his life whenever he sees the Cat.

从那以后，猫和老鼠就成了冤家。直到今天，老鼠还做贼心虚，每次看见猫都撒腿就跑，以保住自己的小命。

What Kind of Music Would Cows Appreciate?

Over 2000 years ago, there was a musician in China who enjoyed playing music out in nature, and he wondered if the animals enjoyed hearing it. In modern times, we have scientists who do experiments to find out the effect of music on animals and even plants, but this was rare in ancient times.

对牛弹琴

二千多年前，中国有一位喜欢在野外演奏的音乐家。他很想看看动物会不会喜欢他的音乐。今天，不少科学家都在试验音乐对动物、甚至植物有什么影响，不过在古代，这样的试验是很少见的。

This musician played a string instrument called *qin*. People loved his music just as much as people today love Yoyo Ma's cello music. On a beautiful spring day, he brought his *qin* to a field where cows were grazing and started playing for them. Pretty soon, people dropped what they were doing and gathered around him. But the cows continued grazing, as though they didn't hear a thing.

A man in front said to the musician, "You are wasting your beautiful music on these stupid cows! How can they understand music?"

这位音乐家演奏的乐器叫作"琴"。他的音乐十分招人喜爱，就像今天人人都爱马友友的大提琴乐曲一样。在一个晴朗的春日里，音乐家带着琴到了郊外，看见一群牛在吃草，他就为这些牛弹起琴来了。不一会儿，人们都停下手里的活儿，凑到音乐家周围。但是牛继续低头吃草，好像什么都没听见。

站在前面的一个男子说："那么动听的音乐弹给这些蠢牛听，真是浪费时间！它们哪儿听得懂啊？"

The musician replied, "You may be right, but maybe I'm not playing the right kind of music. Let me try something else." Then he started playing a strange tune that sounded like calves braying. The crowd of people thought the *qin* had suddenly gone out of tune, and some of them covered up their ears. But almost immediately, all the cows perked up their ears and started shuffling around, as though they were looking for their calves. Soon they all trotted toward the musician, then stood still with their ears perked. Everyone was amazed to see the effect of this strange music on the cows!

音乐家说:"你说的可能有道理,不过也可能是我弹的曲子不合她们的口味,让我试试另一个曲子。"接着,音乐家弹了一个奇怪的调调,听起来就像小牛犊在哞哞地叫。大家都以为是琴突然跑调了,有的人还捂上了耳朵。这时候,只见那些牛都竖起了耳朵,来回走动了起来,好像在找她们的小牛犊。接着,她们都朝音乐家走过来,停下了脚步,竖着耳朵静静地盯着音乐家。大家看到眼前的情景,都很惊讶。

The musician thought to himself, "Wow! Cows do understand music! As long as I understand cows, I can make music they want to hear! How wonderful! I must start making music for other different animals as well!"

音乐家自言自语地说："哇，牛是听得懂音乐的！只要我了解牠们，就能弹出牠们喜欢的音乐，这太棒了！今后我得尝试弹各种不同的曲子，给不同的动物听！"

That day, the musician kept playing the music that sounded like braying calves. He got better and better at it, and pretty soon it became mellow and acquired a rhythm of its own. By this time, those who just didn't get it had left. Those who stayed became captivated, as though they had entered a new musical wonderland.

那天，音乐家一直弹那首像小牛哞哞的曲子，越弹越好，听上去很悦耳又很独特。这时候，那些听不懂的人已经离开了，不过留下来的人都听得入了神，好像进入了一个新的音乐仙境。

How the Tiger Lost His Might

Once upon a time, in a deep forest there lived many lovable animals. Life should have been good for them, but in fact they lived in constant fear of a ferocious tiger. Whenever an animal disappeared, everyone knew that it had fallen into the deadly claws of the tiger. No one was as strong and fierce as this tiger, but there was one—the fox—who was smarter. This fox knew how to hide from the tiger, but he couldn't bear to see his friends disappear one by one. So he came up with a daring plan.

狐假虎威

从前，在一片密密的森林里住着很多可爱的动物。对牠们来说，生活应该很美好，不过因为森林里有一只凶猛的老虎，大家都总是提心吊胆的。每当一只动物不见了，大家都知道牠一定又落入了老虎的魔爪。谁都打不过这只老虎啊！然而，有一只聪明的狐狸知道怎么躲开老虎，但牠不忍心看着好朋友一个一个地被老虎吃掉，于是想出了一个大胆的计划。

One day, he strolled along the tiger's usual path, humming cheerily as he went. Suddenly, the tiger pounced on him. Just as the tiger was about to sink his teeth into the fox, the fox spoke up, "Hmph! So you think you can eat me just because you are the king of beasts?! Well, I am the king of kings sent down by the Heavenly Emperor. Whoever eats me will have to answer to him!" The tiger couldn't believe what he just heard, but the fox's self-assurance made him hesitate. In that moment, the fox knew that his plan was working. So he puffed himself up even more and said "What—you don't believe me? Just follow me, and watch everybody run for their life when they see me coming." The tiger wanted to see this for himself, so he agreed.

有一天，狐狸慢慢地走在老虎平常散步的路上，边走边哼着小曲。突然，老虎蹦了出来，大魔爪抓住了狐狸。老虎张开大嘴，正要咬狐狸的时候，狐狸说话了："哼，你以为自己是百兽之王就可以吃我吗？！告诉你，我是玉皇大帝派来的王中之王，谁吃了我都一定会受到玉皇大帝的惩罚！"老虎听了一惊，不太相信自己的耳朵，但看着狐狸一副自信满满的样子，就犹豫了起来。狐狸知道自己的计谋生效了，所以就更加自信地说："怎么，你不信？那跟着我，让你看看大家一看见我就吓得逃之夭夭了。"老虎心想，那我就去见识见识吧，于是就同意跟着狐狸走一趟。

So, the fox strutted ahead with bold steps, while the tiger tiptoed behind him. As they walked through the woods, all the animals ran for their lives when they saw the tiger coming. Thereupon, the fox turned to the tiger and said, "See? Didn't I tell you?" "Sure enough, Your Majesty!" said the tiger, for he had no idea that it was he, and not the fox, who had scared all the other animals.

就这样，狐狸昂首挺胸地走在前头，老虎小心翼翼地跟在后头。牠们俩穿过森林的时候，其他动物看见老虎来了，都吓得四处奔逃。狐狸回过头对老虎说："看见了吧？我说什么来着？"老虎赶紧说："是的，陛下，您说的没错！"老虎根本不知道那些动物是看见走在狐狸后头的牠才吓得飞奔逃命的。

Ever since then, all the animals knew they were safe as long as they stayed close to the fox. As for the tiger, his tiger nature did not change one bit, but he has learned to stay away from the fox's neck of the woods.

从那以后，大家都知道只要跟狐狸在一起就不用怕那只老虎了。而老虎呢，本性一点儿没变，不过牠也不敢再到狐狸的地盘上去了。

How an Old Rabbit Saved Her Forest Friends

There once was a beautiful forest where many different animals lived, including chipmunks, snakes, monkeys, owls, foxes, and rabbits. They lived together like one big happy family.

In this forest, there was an old well. Once a bunny looked in it and saw another bunny. Thinking that this bunny could be a playmate, he jumped in and drowned. Since then, all the animals in the forest taught their children to stay away from the well.

老兔英雄

很久以前，在一片美丽的森林里住着很多不同的动物，有花栗鼠、蛇、猴子、猫头鹰、狐狸和兔子。牠们就像一个大家庭，一起生活得很开心。

森林里有一口老井。有一次，一只小兔在井边往下看，看见另一只小兔，以为终于有个玩伴了，一高兴就跳了下去，结果淹死了。从那以后，动物爸妈们都告诫自己的孩子必须远离那口井。

One day, the forest became a dangerous place. A lion discovered this beautiful forest, with all his favorite preys to feed on. So he moved right in and declared himself the King. All the animals were terrified. The elders of the forest decided to bargain with the lion, to keep the forest as safe as possible.

The lion came right to the point: "As you all know, lions are ferocious hunters. But I'm nicer than other lions. I only need to eat one animal a day. If one of you would sacrifice yourself each day, I promise to spare your babies." This was still a terrible deal, but the elders felt it was the best they could do.

有一天，一头狮子发现了这块风水宝地，这里就不再安宁了。森林里有那么多的小动物可以让狮子大饱口福，牠马上大摇大摆地进来了，并宣布自己是森林之王。动物们都吓坏了，一些长辈们决定跟狮子谈判，尽可能保护好小动物们。

狮子一开口就说："你们都知道，狮子是凶猛的猎兽。不过，我比其他的狮子好一点儿，每天只要吃一只动物就够了。你们当中谁要自愿牺牲自己，我保证不伤害你们的孩子。"虽然狮子的提议还是挺恐怖的，但是长辈们也想不出更好的办法来了。

After the lion left, the elders formed a circle and made this decision: Since they were old and would die soon anyway, they might as well be the ones to be sacrificed. So they agreed to draw lots each day to decide who would be the lion's meal.

Then Old Rabbit said: "Since I'm the oldest and don't have children to care for anymore, I'll volunteer to be the first meal for the lion." All the others started to cry. Then she added, "I'm sorry to make you sad, but thank you for agreeing to this best possible solution."

When Old Rabbit arrived at the lion's home, she was huffing and puffing from having run too fast. Before the lion could pounce on her, she said, "I saw another lion on my way here, so I ran with all my might so I wouldn't be killed before I could reach you."

狮子走了以后，长辈们围坐在一起，做了一个决定：牠们都老了，早晚都会死的，不如就牺牲自己吧。因此，牠们决定每天抽签来决定谁不幸地成为狮子的盘中餐。

这时候，老兔子开口说："我的年龄最大，也没有孩子要照顾了，所以就让我去做狮子的第一餐吧。"所有的动物听了都哭了起来，老兔子又说，"我真不想让大家难过…不过我们没有更好的办法了…谢谢大家接受我的建议。"

老兔子到狮子家的时候，跑得气喘吁吁的。狮子刚要扑上去，就听见老兔子说："刚才在来的路上看见了另一头狮子，我拼命地跑才没被牠吃掉。"

The lion was shocked: "What?! I thought I was the only lion in this forest, and I would be the King! Take me to this other lion and I'll show him who is King!"

Old Rabbit led the lion to the well and told him the other lion lived in there. The lion looked in and roared at his reflection. He became really furious when the lion in the well roared back, so he jumped right in to attack it, and that was the end of him!

Old Rabbit was declared Queen of the forest. After she passed away at a ripe old age, the well was turned into the Rabbit Memorial, and you can still see it there today.

狮子大吃一惊："什么?！我不是这片森林里唯一的狮子王吗？你马上带我去找那头狮子，好让牠知道谁是真正的大王！"

老兔子把狮子带到了老井边上，说另一头狮子就在下面。狮子往下一看，张开大嘴对着下面的狮子咆哮了起来。下面的狮子也对着牠咆哮起来，这让牠更生气了，立刻跳了下去收拾那头狮子，活该牠就这样呜呼哀哉了！

所有的动物都欢呼雀跃，推选老兔子为森林女王。过了几年，老兔子去世了以后，那口老井就变成了"老兔纪念碑"，到今天还能看见呢。

How to Make Dragons Come to Life

About 1500 years ago, there was an artist in China famous for making animals look alive on paintings. The emperor hired him to paint four dragons on a wall at a temple. He finished the job very quickly. When a crowd gathered to admire the wall, everyone said the dragons looked so lifelike that they could practically fly off the wall. But when the emperor took a closeup look, he noticed that the dragons had no eyes. The artist explained that if he put on the eyes, the dragons would really come to life and fly away. The emperor didn't believe him and insisted that he add the eyes.

画龙点睛

大约1500年前，中国有一位画家画的动物栩栩如生。皇帝请他在一座寺庙的墙壁上画四条龙。画家没过几天就完工了。那天，人们围在壁画前，欣赏画家的大作。大家都说那四条龙看上去生动得好像要从壁画上飞起来了。不过，皇帝仔细一看，发现那四条龙都没有眼睛。画家告诉皇帝，要是给龙画上眼睛，龙就会活起来，真的会飞走的。皇帝不信，坚持要画家把龙的眼睛画上。

As the artist picked up his brush and started adding eyes on the dragons, dark clouds loomed overhead, followed by gusts of wind, then a flash of lightning and a clap of thunder. Then the two dragons that had been given eyes started wiggling on the wall, then soared up into the stormy sky! The emperor was amazed. "Stop! Stop!" he shouted. "Don't put eyes on the other two dragons!" Soon, the storm blew over and the clouds cleared up. When the crowd looked at the wall again, sure enough, only the two dragons without eyes remained.

画家拿起了画笔，开始给龙画上眼睛。这时候，乌云滚滚、疾风阵阵、电闪雷鸣。只见壁画上画上了眼睛的两条龙扭动着身子，嗖的一声冲进了风雨交加的天空！皇帝大吃一惊，大叫了起来："快停下来，别画了！别给另外两条龙画眼睛了！"这时，暴风雨停了，云雾也散了。大家再一看壁画，上面只剩下两条还没画上眼睛的龙了。

How to Make Dragons Come to Life

Can this story be true? Well, it is true that there was such a wonderful artist who painted all kinds of creatures, including dragons. The part about the dragons flying off the wall can't be true, but we call it a "metaphor" rather than a lie. A metaphor is a colorful way to say something. So "putting eyes on a dragon" actually means "putting the final touches on a piece of art to make it come to life." In writing a story, you can use this metaphor to mean "ending the story with a perfect finale." In describing a great teacher, we might use the metaphor "She can light a fire under her students." When a student answers a question perfectly, this teacher might say "You hit the bullseye!" Now can you make up a metaphor of your own?

这个故事是真的吗？嗯，历史上确实有这么一位了不起的画家，画各种动物，当然也画龙。不过故事里说的"壁画上的两条龙活起来了"当然不是真的，但是我们把这种写作手法叫作"比喻"，而不是撒谎。比喻是一种生动有趣的叙事方法。因此，"画龙点睛"的意思就是"给一件艺术作品添加最生动的一笔，让它栩栩如生。"写一个故事的时候，"画龙点睛"的比喻就是"给故事写了一个完美的结尾。"对于一位可以激发学生学习热情的优秀教师，我们可以比喻为"能点燃学生心中的火花。"当一个学生给出完全正确的回答时，老师可以比喻说："你的回答击中了靶心！"现在，你自己能不能想出一个好的比喻来呢？

Would You Save a Snake from Freezing to Death?

There once was a farmer who lived in a village with his wife and two children. He was the kindest man in the world. Not only was he kind to all his friends and neighbors, he was also kind to troublesome people and even vicious animals. On a frosty winter day, on his way home from working in the fields, he saw a snake curled up on the side of the road, frozen stiff as though it was near death. He picked it up and put it inside his jacket to warm it back to life.

善良的农夫与蛇

很久以前，有个农夫和妻子带着两个孩子住在一个村子里。人们都觉得农夫是世界上最善良的人，不但对朋友和乡亲们很友好，甚至对那些讨厌的人和恶毒的动物也充满爱心。在一个寒冷的冬日里，农夫干完地里的活儿，走在回家的路上，突然看见路边蜷缩着一条蛇。那条蛇看起来冻僵了，快要死了。农夫把蛇捡起来，解开外衣，把牠放进了怀里。农夫想用自己的体温来救活这条蛇。

When the snake revived and regained its strength, it promptly bit the farmer on his chest. The farmer stumbled his way home and collapsed just as he entered his cottage. Alas, the snake turned out to be poisonous! As the farmer lay dying, he said to his family, "It's too late to save me now, but learn from my mistake: be kind, but think twice before you do a kind deed for someone who might be vicious."

过了一会儿，蛇慢慢地醒了，又有了力气，就猛地在农夫的胸口上咬了一口。农夫跌跌撞撞地往家里走去，一回到自己的小屋里就瘫倒在了地上。太糟了，原来那是一条毒蛇！农夫快要断气的时候，告诉家人："我没救了，不过你们要记住我的教训：做人要善良，但是做善事以前，一定得看清楚你想帮助的是不是个坏蛋啊！"

Dear reader, we don't like this tragic ending, do we? So, let's rewrite the second half of the story. Please read on!

亲爱的读者，这个故事的后一半是不是太悲伤了？我们把它变得快乐一点，好不好？继续往下看吧！

Arriving at his cottage, the farmer gently laid the stiff snake near the warm fireplace. When the snake woke up, it felt hungry and looked around for something to eat. Soon it saw several puppies huddled around the family dog in the corner of the room. As it slithered toward the puppies, it let out a threatening hiss, which alarmed the farmer. Seeing what the snake was about to do, the farmer ran for his ax and quickly chopped off the snake's head. As the snake lay dying, the farmer said, "I am sad to kill any living creature, but if you are so harmful to others, I should never have saved you!" Then he turned to his family and said, "This was a valuable lesson for us all: Be kind, but think twice before you do a kind deed for someone who might be vicious."

农夫到家以后，把蛇轻轻地放在了温暖的壁炉边上，让牠暖和暖和。过了一会儿，蛇慢慢地醒了过来。牠觉得肚子有点饿，就左右看看，想找一点儿东西吃。牠看见墙角那里的狗妈妈身边趴着几只刚出生的狗宝宝，就开始往那边爬过去。这时候，农夫听到蛇发出的嘶嘶声，看见牠快要咬到狗宝宝了，就拿起一把斧头，一下子把蛇的头砍了下来。农夫看着死了的蛇说："我真的不想杀生，但是你这个害人的家伙，我真不该救你啊！"然后转身对家人说："这对我们都是个教训：做人要善良，但是做善事以前，一定得看清楚你想帮助的是不是个坏蛋啊！"

Can Losing a Horse Bring Good Luck?

About 2000 years ago, more and more Chinese people moved to the northern frontier of China. Here they came into contact with the nomadic tribes that roamed the area. Sometimes they lived side-by-side peacefully, sometimes not.

塞翁失马

大约2000年前，很多中国人迁移到了北部的边境，跟那里的游牧民族有了接触。他们有时候和平共处，但有时候也会发生冲突。

In one of these frontier villages, there lived an old man who had only a son and a horse as his family. One day, his horse disappeared. Everyone thought it either wandered over to the nomads' area or was in fact stolen by the nomads. The old man's friends came to console him, but they were surprised to hear him say: "How do we know this is not a blessing in disguise?" Sure enough, a couple of weeks later, his horse came home, bringing with it a sprightly mare. Now everyone thought the horse had gone off and found himself a mate, so they came to congratulate the old man. But the old man replied, "How do we know this is not a tragedy in the making?"

在边境的一个村子里住着一个老人，他的妻子早就去世了，家里只有一个儿子和一匹马。有一天，马不见了。乡亲们都觉得马可能跑到游牧人住的地方去了，也有可能是被游牧人偷走了！大家都来安慰老人，可没想到他居然说："谁知道这不是一件好事呢？"果然，几个星期以后，老人的马回来了，还带回来了一匹漂亮的母马！大家都说老人的马一定是跑到境外去了，还给自己找回来一个伴儿！朋友们又来恭喜老人，但他又说："谁知道这不是一件坏事呢？"

Just a couple of days later, disaster struck! The old man's son loved to ride horses, but the mare had never been trained. When the young man mounted her, she reared up and threw him to the ground. He heard his right leg snap, then felt a shooting pain. Alas, this accident crippled him for the rest of his life. The old man's friends again came to console him. This time they were not too surprised to hear him say, "How do we know this is not a blessing in disguise?"

过了几天果然又出事儿了！老人的儿子很喜欢骑马，不过那匹母马从来没被训练过。年轻人一骑到牠背上，牠就高高地抬起前蹄，把年轻人重重地摔到了地上。他听见自己的右腿咯吱一声，然后感觉到一阵阵剧痛。唉，这一摔让他从今以后就成了一个残疾人。朋友们又来安慰老人，但他还是说："谁知道这不是一件好事儿呢？"这一次，大家听了都不再惊讶了。

Can Losing a Horse Bring Good Luck?

A year later, war broke out between the nomadic tribes and the Chinese empire. The Chinese emperor called all the able-bodied young men in the villages to fight the nomads. Many of them died in battle. The old man's son, crippled from his fall, did not join the war and lived on.

To this day, when trouble befalls a Chinese person, his friends may remind him that it may be a blessing in disguise, just like the old man who lost his horse.

一年后，中国和游牧部落打起仗来了。中国的皇帝要村子里所有的壮丁都去打仗，结果很多人都战死了。老人的儿子因为前一年从马背上摔下来，成了残疾人，就没有被送去打仗，所以活下来了。

今天，中国人遇到不幸的事情的时候，朋友们往往会用"塞翁失马"这个故事来安慰他。

Why Bother Repairing the Fence After the Sheep Are Already Lost?

Once there was a shepherd who lived at the edge of a Chinese village. He was not so bright, but his kind neighbor, a carpenter, was always willing to help him. The shepherd had one dozen sheep, and he counted them twice a day—once in the morning when he took them out to pasture, and once in the afternoon when he brought them home. One morning, he was surprised to find that there were only eleven sheep.

亡羊补牢

从前，在中国的一个村子边上住着一个牧羊人。他有一点儿笨，但幸好有个善良的木匠邻居，总是乐意帮他的忙。牧羊人养了12只羊，每天都把这些羊数两遍：早上出去放牧的时候跟下午把羊赶回羊圈的时候各数一遍。有一天早上，他发现少了一只羊，就有点惊慌。

He went to ask his neighbor, "Did you happen to see anyone sneak into the pen last night to steal one of my sheep?"

"No way!" said the carpenter, "We are a small village where no one ever locks a door. Did you check the fence to see if it's broken anywhere?"

The shepherd just wanted to find his lost sheep and didn't think checking the fence would do any good. The next morning, he discovered that another sheep was gone. When it happened again on the third day, he told his friend that he would ask other villagers if they saw anything. That's when the carpenter offered to come take a look at the fence.

他跑去问邻居："你昨天晚上有没有看见什么人溜进了我的羊圈，偷走了一只羊？"

"不可能吧！"木匠说，"村子里大家的房门都不上锁，哪儿来的贼呢？你有没有检查自己的羊圈，看看栅栏是不是坏了？"

牧羊人一心只想找到丢失的羊，不觉得检查栅栏有什么用，所以就没听木匠的话。第二天，他发现又少了一只羊，第三天又有一只羊不见了。他对木匠说，"我去问问老乡们，看他们知不知道是怎么回事儿。"这时候，木匠就决定过去看看羊圈的栅栏。

As they went into the pen, the carpenter noticed right away that there were some unusual tracks on the ground. After a moment of thought, he gasped, "Oh my god! These are wolf tracks!" Then he noticed a few broken slats on the fence, but the hole didn't look big enough for a wolf to get through. As he got closer though, he saw that a big hole was dug in the ground below the broken slats! "Wow!" he exclaimed, "This wolf is really sneaky! It made the hole in the fence so small that people wouldn't see it!"

　他们俩一走进羊圈，木匠就注意到地上有一些奇特的脚印。他想了一下，就惊叫起来："天哪，羊圈里进来了狼了！"后来，他看到栅栏上的几根木条坏了，但那个洞不太大，狼应该进不来。木匠走到跟前再仔细一看，原来坏了的木条下面，地上有个大洞！他又惊叫了一声："天哪，这只狼太狡猾了！牠把栅栏上的洞弄得很小，人们很难发现地上那个大洞！"

Thinking that the wolf may return again that night, the two of them repaired the fence that very day. While they were at it, they extended the fence deeper into the ground, so the wolf couldn't sneak into the pen anymore. Having learned a lesson the hard way, the shepherd promised himself that he would always listen to his friend's advice the first time around.

想着狼很可能当天晚上还会回来，牧羊人和木匠就赶紧把羊圈修好了，还把栅栏的木条往地下加深了一些，这样狼就不可能偷爬进来了。牧羊人觉得这件事儿给了他一个惨痛的教训，就告诫自己今后要从一开始就好好听朋友的劝告。

How the Monkey Was Doomed by His Own Pride

Sailors in ancient Greece often kept a monkey onboard because monkeys were enjoyable company. The monkeys were happy with this arrangement, because they got to see many interesting places around the Mediterranean Sea. Because they could climb easily to the top of the ship's mast, they were usually the first ones to spot the interesting things from afar. As you can imagine, these monkeys felt they were on top of the world, and became quite proud of themselves, in fact too proud for their own good.

猴子与海豚

在古希腊，海员们出海的时候往往在船上带着一只猴子，给他们添一些乐趣。这些猴子有机会环游地中海周边许多有趣的地方也觉得很开心。因为猴子很容易就能爬到船桅的顶端，所以他们总能最先发现远处有意思的东西。可想而知，这些猴子觉得他们"高高在上"就变得非常骄傲，甚至有点得意忘形了。

Sailing is a wonderful adventure, but in the bad old days, shipwrecks happened quite often. During the height of the Greek empire, a ship sailing from Corinth to Athens was caught in a terrible storm as it neared the harbor. The ship capsized and everyone was thrown overboard. The only way they could save themselves was to swim for land, and many of them did not make it.

航海可让人心旷神怡，但风险也很大。在古代，航海常常发生翻船的海难。在希腊最强盛的时候，有一次，一艘从科林斯开往雅典的海船在快要到达港口的时候遇到了一场大的暴风雨。船翻了，所有的人都落进了海里。他们只有拼命地游到岸边才能活命，但很多人都没能上岸。

The monkey on this ship was lucky that a dolphin saw him thrashing in the water. The dolphin mistook the monkey for a man, and quickly lifted him on his back to carry him to shore. To help his new friend relax, the dolphin started some chitchat:

"On your way home from a trip?"

"Oh yes," the monkey piped up, "I often sail to other islands on business, and we just wrapped up a deal in Corinth. Our family have been Athenians for generations, in fact, we were among the first families of our magnificent city."

这艘船上的猴子很幸运，因为一只海豚看见牠在水里扑腾，以为是个海员，就飞快地游过去，把牠托在了背上，往岸边游去。为了让新朋友放松一点儿，海豚就跟牠聊起天儿来：

"你出海回家来了？"

"对啊，"猴子开始夸夸其谈起来，"我常常出海，到其他岛屿去做生意，这次刚在科林斯做了一笔大生意。我的家族世世代代都是雅典人，实际上，我的祖先是宏伟雅典的创始人之一呢！"

"Then, of course, you must know Piraeus well," said the dolphin.

"Oh, yes," said the monkey, thinking that Piraeus was some distinguished Athenian citizen, "he is one of my best friends."

This reply from the monkey didn't make sense at all, because Piraeus was not a person's name, but the famous port city near Athens. The dolphin turned his head to look, and was shocked to see that the person on his back was actually a monkey! Realizing that he had been tricked, he quickly dived to the bottom of the sea, and left the bluffing monkey to his fate.

"是吗？那你一定对比雷埃夫斯很熟悉吧？"海豚说。

"当然咯，"猴子以为比雷埃夫斯是某个高贵的雅典公民，就跟海豚说："他是我最好的朋友之一呢！"

海豚听了猴子的回答，觉得很奇怪。比雷埃夫斯根本不是一个人的名字，而是雅典附近一个有名的港口。海豚回头一看，惊讶地发现牠背上不是一个人，而是一只猴子！这时候海豚才知道自己被骗了，所以牠一头扎进了海底，让爱吹牛的猴子听天由命去吧！

Why the Hen that Laid Golden Eggs Couldn't Save Herself

There once was a humble young couple who made their living by raising hens and selling eggs in the market. They earned enough money to get by, but they wished they could be richer. By and by, they noticed that the eggs from a hen named Blackie were bigger than all the others. They decided to feed Blackie more to see if her eggs could get big enough to sell at a higher price. Sure enough, Blackie started laying bigger and bigger eggs. One day, a miracle happened! The egg Blackie laid was made of gold! This continued for a week.

杀鸡取卵

从前，有一对老实的年轻夫妻靠养鸡，在集市上卖鸡蛋生活。他们的日子过得还不错，但总希望能更富有。有一天，他们发现一只叫"小黑"的母鸡下的蛋比其他的都大，就想让小黑多吃一些，下更大的蛋，卖更多的钱。果然，小黑下的蛋越来越大。有一天，奇迹出现了！小黑下了一只金蛋！在后来的一个星期里，小黑每天都下一个金蛋。

The couple was overjoyed! Then they got an idea: "Hmm..., one golden egg from Blackie is worth a lot more than the eggs from all the other hens. Why not sell all the other hens at the market?" As the hens were being taken to market the next day, they ganged up and squawked, "Don't sell us, or you'll be sorry!" Their pleas fell on deaf ears.

　　夫妻二人高兴极了！心想："嗯…，小黑下的一个金蛋比别的鸡下的蛋都更值钱，不如把别的鸡都拿到集市上去卖了？"第二天，夫妻二人把那些鸡带到集市去的路上，鸡们都嘎嘎地说："求求你们，别把我们卖了，不然你们会后悔的！"夫妻二人假装什么都没听见。

As the couple became rich, they became lazier and lazier. Soon they bought a big house, fancy clothes, and a fancy car. They began wishing to travel the world, but they couldn't very well take Blackie along. One day, the husband came up with an idea: "Since Blackie drops one golden egg each day, she must have many more in her, enough to support us for the rest of our life. Why not get all the gold out of her now, and we wouldn't have to take care of her anymore."

后来，夫妻二人越来越有钱，不过也变得越来越懒。他们很快就买了大房子，漂亮的衣服，还有一辆豪车。他们开始想到世界各地去旅游，可是小黑怎么办呢？没办法带着牠一起周游世界啊！有一天，丈夫有了个主意："既然小黑每天都下一个金蛋，牠肚子里一定还有很多金蛋，我们一辈子都吃不完用不尽。不如我们现在就把牠肚子里的金蛋都拿出来，以后就不用再管牠了。"

The couple decided to carry out this plan the next day. Blackie protested with all her might, but it was useless. As the man raised the chopping knife, Blackie screamed, "You ingrates! You will get what you deserve!" Well, the inside of Blackie turned out to be no different from any other hen, just a mess of guts.

第二天，夫妻二人决定杀了小黑取金蛋。小黑拼命反抗，但没有用。丈夫举起菜刀的时候，小黑大叫道："你们真没良心啊，会遭报应的！"夫妻二人打开小黑的肚子一看，里面根本没有金蛋，跟别的母鸡一样，只有一堆乱七八糟的内脏。

Having sold all their other hens, the couple had no way to earn any money, and their wealth dwindled quickly. Soon, they had to sell everything they owned to buy food. In the end, they became beggars in the marketplace. All the villagers knew they had no mercy for their hens, so no one took pity on them.

因为夫妻二人已经把别的母鸡都卖了，现在没办法赚钱了，原来的钱也很快用光了。没过多久，他们就为了吃饭而卖掉了所有的东西。最后，他们只好在集市上讨饭去了。村子里的人都知道他们没有良心，对那些母鸡那么残忍，所以没有人同情他们。

Are Dogs Really Happier Than Wolves?

Once during a drought in ancient Greece, a lean and hungry wolf came to town looking for creatures to eat. There he met a dog who looked like a distant relative, so he chatted her up.

"Long time no see, my friend! How have you been all these years?"

狼 与 狗 的 对 话

古希腊有一年发生了大旱灾，一只又瘦又饿的狼进城来找些可吃的小动物。牠遇见了一条狗，觉得很像自己的一个远亲，就跟牠聊了起来。

"好久不见，老朋友！这些年你过得怎么样啊？"

The dog was embarrassed that she didn't remember this "old friend," but decided to pretend she did, so she replied, "Not bad! As you can see, I live in a nice house and my master feeds me very well. All I have to do is to guard the house at night."

"Lucky you! As for me, life in the woods is not bad. I can usually find plenty of game to feed on. But it hasn't rained for six months, and all the animals in the wild are starving to death. So I came to town to see what I can find here. Since we're related, maybe you can give me some ideas!"

"No problem, my friend! Just come with me and I'll introduce you to my master as my new pal."

狗没认出来这个"老朋友"，觉得有点不好意思，但又不想让狼看出来，所以就说："挺好的！你看，我住着漂亮的房子，每天享受着主人喂我的美食，我只要晚上把家门看好就行了。"

"真羡慕你啊！我呢，在树林里的生活也不错，通常都能找到不少小猎物，但最近六个月都没下雨，树林里的动物都饿死了，所以我才进城来找点吃的。既然我们是亲戚，你帮我出出主意呗？"

"好啊，老朋友！那你跟我来吧，我把你介绍给我的主人，就说你是我的新朋友吧！"

Just then, the wolf noticed a ring around the dog's neck, so he asked if it's a necklace.

"Oh no," the dog replied, "My master put this collar on me when I was a puppy. Whenever he takes me out, he puts a leash on it to make sure I don't wander away."

"What?! A leash?!" cried the wolf in shock, "You mean you are not allowed to roam wherever you please?"

"Well, you see, people who don't know me might think I'm ferocious. The leash helps everyone feel safe. Once you get used to it, you'd be happy to just go wherever your master goes!"

这时候，狼看见狗的脖子上套着一个圆圈，就问那是不是一条项链。

"噢，不是的，"狗解释道，"我还很小的时候，主人就给我戴上了这个项圈。每次出门的时候，主人把一根狗绳系在项圈上，这样我就不会走远了。"

"什么？！系一根狗绳？！"狼惊讶地大叫了起来，"难道你不能自由地走来走去吗？"

"嗯，你看，不认识我的人可能会以为我很凶猛，但我系上狗绳以后，大家就安心了。我早就习惯了，主人想去哪儿，我就跟着他去哪儿，这样也挺开心的。"

"Whew! I'm so glad my ancestors didn't get lured into becoming man's best friend! I would never trade my freedom for all the luxury in the world!" With this, the wolf dashed back into the woods!

The dog thought for a moment, then said to herself, "He's got a point. This might be what my master means when he says 'you can't eat your cake and have it too.'"

"哎呀，幸亏当年我的祖先没像你的那样上当受骗，成为了人类的'挚友'！人间的任何荣华富贵都抵不过我的自由！"说完，狼一溜烟就跑回树林里去了！

狗低头想了一会儿，自言自语地说："狼说的也有道理，这可能就是主人说的'鱼与熊掌不可兼得'吧！"

How Piggy Learned an Unforgettable Lesson

About 1400 years ago, a Chinese monk went on a pilgrimage with his three disciples: the clever Monkey, the naughty Piggy, and a fellow named Sandy.

One day, trekking through a desert, the travelers became tired and thirsty. Monkey —who has a magic cape that could quickly take him to anywhere in the world— volunteered to go find tropical fruit. He agreed to let Piggy tag along, even though he knew this would mean trouble.

猪八戒吃西瓜

大约1400年前，唐僧到西天去取经的时候，带了三个徒弟：孙悟空、猪八戒和沙僧。

有一天，师徒四人穿过一片沙漠，走得又累又渴。悟空出了个主意：因为他身上穿着一件魔力斗篷，翻一个跟斗就可以去到很远的地方，可以替大家去找一些热带水果回来。八戒吵着要跟着去，悟空明知八戒会惹麻烦，不过还是答应了。

Sure enough, soon after they started, Piggy got tired and wanted to rest under a tree. There was no time to waste, so Monkey said, "I'll just go myself, and pick you up later." Then he unfurled his magic cape and off he went.

As Piggy settled down to take a nap, he saw a watermelon at the bottom of the hill, then he noticed some wheel tracks on the ground. "Aha!" he thought, "This melon must have rolled off some traveler's cart! I'll take it to share with everybody right away!" But on second thought, he decided to cut it open and eat his share right away. It tasted so good that he couldn't stop at just one piece. Before long, he ate up the other three pieces as well.

果然，两人刚走了一会儿，八戒就累了，要在树下休息。悟空不想浪费时间，就对八戒说："我先去找水果，回头来接你。"说完，悟空一掀斗篷，腾空而去。

八戒刚躺下要小睡一会儿，就看见山脚下有一个西瓜，还注意到地上有一些车轱辘印。"哈，西瓜一定是从过路的车上掉下来的！我快去捡来，跟大家一起分享！"这时八戒又犹豫了一下，决定先吃了自己的那一份。西瓜太好吃了，八戒根本停不下来。不一会儿，整个西瓜都进了牠圆圆的肚子了。

Suddenly, he heard Monkey calling "Piggy, I'm back!" Alarmed, he flung the pieces of watermelon rind as far as he could. Actually, from above the clouds, Monkey had already seen what Piggy did with the watermelon. But pretending that he saw nothing, he said, "Let's go, Piggy, I've got plenty of tropical fruit for everybody!"

The two ran as fast as they could, but Monkey led Piggy along the path strewn with the watermelon rind. Piggy suddenly went "kapunk!" as he fell on something slippery. This happened again, and again, and again! He fell so hard that he was covered with scrapes and bruises by the time they arrived.

这时候，八戒听见悟空大喊一声："八戒，我回来了！"八戒吓了一跳，赶紧把一堆西瓜皮往远处扔。其实，悟空在天上已经看见八戒偷吃了西瓜。不过，悟空假装什么都不知道，跟八戒说："走吧，看我找到了那么多热带水果！"

八戒和悟空就赶紧上路了，不过悟空故意带着八戒奔跑在满是西瓜皮的路上。只听见"哧溜"一声，八戒踩到了一块西瓜皮，四脚朝天摔倒在了地上。刚站起来，又踩到了另一块，就这样接二连三滑倒了好几次！等牠们回到原先的地方，可怜的八戒身上已经青一块紫一块了。

The monk was delighted to see Monkey and Piggy return with the tropical fruit, but the first thing he said was, "What ever happened to you, Piggy?!"

Piggy was too ashamed of himself to tell the whole story, so he just muttered, "I learned a lesson that I will never forget." At that, everyone looked at him with a kindly smile.

"Glad to hear it!" said the monk, "Now let's all have some delicious fruit to celebrate!"

看到悟空和八戒带着那么多热带水果回来，唐僧很高兴，不过他说的第一句话是："八戒，你怎么了？"

八戒很羞愧，没脸告诉大家牠偷吃了西瓜，就支支吾吾地说："我学到了一个永远忘不了的教训。"另外三人听了，都会心地一笑。

"那好极了！"唐僧说："看！那么多美味的水果！大家快来一起吃个痛快吧！"

"Books to Span the East and West"

Tuttle Publishing was founded in 1832 in the small New England town of Rutland, Vermont [USA]. Our core values remain as strong today as they were then—to publish best-in-class books which bring people together one page at a time. In 1948, we established a publishing outpost in Japan—and Tuttle is now a leader in publishing English-language books about the arts, languages and cultures of Asia. The world has become a much smaller place today and Asia's economic and cultural influence has grown. Yet the need for meaningful dialogue and information about this diverse region has never been greater. Over the past seven decades, Tuttle has published thousands of books on subjects ranging from martial arts and paper crafts to language learning and literature— and our talented authors, illustrators, designers and photographers have won many prestigious awards. We welcome you to explore the wealth of information available on Asia at **www.tuttlepublishing.com.**

Published by Tuttle Publishing, an imprint of
Periplus Editions (HK) Ltd.

www.tuttlepublishing.com

Text© 2023 Vivian Ling & Wang Peng
Illustrations© 2023 Yang Xi

Isbn: 978-0-8048-5594-5

Library of Congress Cataloging-in-Publication Data in process

26 25 24 23   10 9 8 7 6 5 4 3 2 1
Printed in China   2305EP

Distributed by

North America, Latin America & Europe
Tuttle Publishing
364 Innovation Drive
North Clarendon, VT 05759-9436 U.S.A.
Tel: 1 (802) 773-8930
Fax: 1 (802) 773-6993
info@tuttlepublishing.com
www.tuttlepublishing.com

Asia Pacific
Berkeley Books Pte. Ltd.
3 Kallang Sector #04-01
Singapore 349278
Tel: (65) 6741 2178
Fax: (65) 6741 2179
inquiries@periplus.com.sg
www.tuttlepublishing.com

How to access the online recordings for this book:

1. Check to be sure you have an internet connection.
2. Type the following URL into your web browser:
https://www.tuttlepublishing.com/the-twelve-animals-of-the-chinese-zodiac

For support you can email us at:
info@tuttlepublishing.com